The
Reluctant
Dragon

Kenneth Grahame
Adapted by Katie Daynes

Illustrated by Fred Blunt

Reading Consultant: Alison Kelly
Roehampton University

One evening,
long ago, a shepherd
ran home, terrified.

2

"It has long,
sharp claws...

a long, pointy
tail...

...and shiny blue
scales all over
its body."

His son looked up
from his book.

"That sounds like a
dragon," he said.

"A dragon?" yelped the wife.

"A *dragon*?" said the shepherd.

"That does not sound good."

The boy wasn't
scared. The next day,
he set off up the hill
to find the
dragon.

Bye. Don't
worry!

"He might be friendly,"
thought the boy.

The dragon *was* friendly – and he was thrilled to see the boy.

It's beautiful here, but it does get lonely.

10

The boy smiled. He sat down and asked the dragon all kinds of questions.

The dragon told stories of long, long ago.

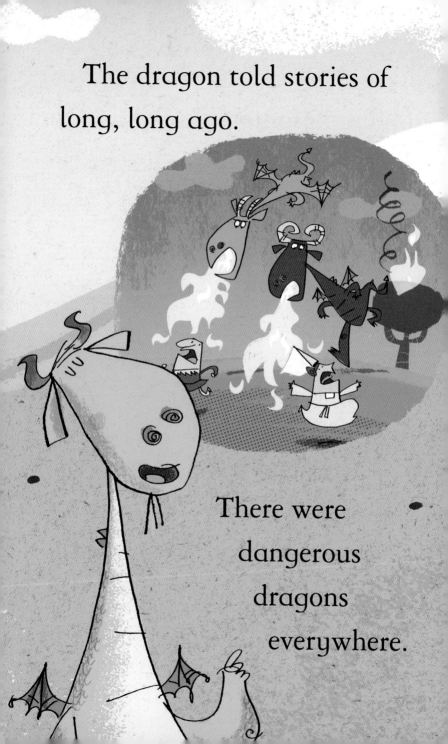

There were dangerous dragons everywhere.

And brave knights fought
them to rescue princesses.

The boy came back every
day to hear the stories.

But then the villagers found out about the dragon. They were terrified.

SLAY THE DRAGON

BAN THE DRAGON

BANISH THE DRAGON

SLAY THE DRAGON

BANISH THE DRAGON

SLAY THE DRAGON

The boy ran straight to the dragon. "The villagers want to get rid of you!" he panted.

But I wouldn't hurt a fly!

That afternoon, the boy
heard even worse news.

He's here!

Who's
here?

Saint George, the Dragon Killer!

He's going to fight the dragon!

The boy rushed back to the dragon.

17

"Saint George the Dragon Killer wants to fight you," gasped the boy.

"I'll just hide in my cave until he goes away," said the dragon.

"You can't!" cried the boy. "Everyone wants a fight!"

The dragon yawned.
"I'm sure you'll think of
something," he said.

The boy walked slowly
back down to the village.

He eats ten sheep
for breakfast.

A crowd of villagers was telling George about the dangerous dragon.

He burned down five houses.

"It's not true!" said the boy.
"The dragon wouldn't hurt
a fly."

"But everyone wants a fight," said George. "What can I do?"

"Follow me," said the boy. And he took George to meet the dragon.

"What a perfect place for a fight," said George. "No fighting," said the dragon, firmly.

"Not even a
pretend fight?"
asked the boy.

"Maybe..."
said the dragon.

27

The boy turned to George.
"Do you promise not to
hurt him?"

"Well, it has to look
real," said George.

"Will there be a feast afterwards?" asked the dragon.

"There will, and you can come," promised George.

29

The next morning,
lots of villagers
arrived to watch
the fight.

The boy waited
nervously by the
dragon's cave.

They cheered and waved when Saint George rode into view. But where was the dragon?

32

Then a roar echoed around
the hills. Flames filled
the air.

Everyone gasped as the dragon appeared. His scales sparkled and he breathed out fire.

"Charge!" cried George.
He galloped hard, his spear
held high.

The dragon bounded up.

And they shot past each other.

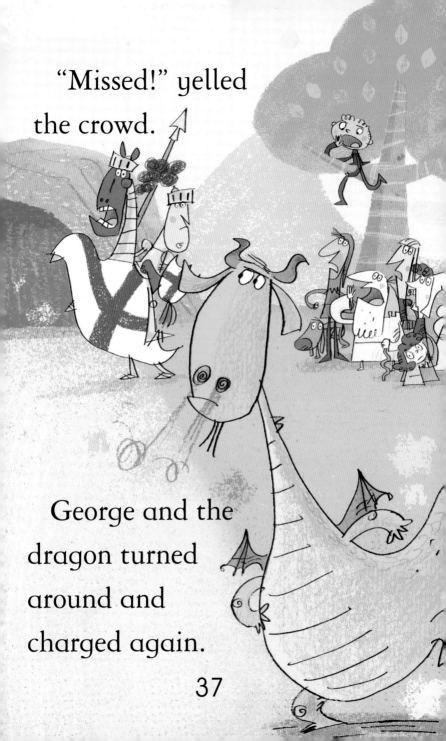

"Missed!" yelled the crowd.

George and the dragon turned around and charged again.

37

This time, there was no
way they could miss.
CLATTER! BANG! OUF!

The dragon slumped to the ground. George towered over him.

Cut off his head!

"I think the dragon
has learned his lesson," George
declared. "Let's invite him
to our feast."

And he led the villagers,
the boy and the dragon back
down the hill.

The boy was happy
because his plan worked.

The villagers were
happy because they'd seen
a fight. George was happy
because he'd won.

The dragon was happiest
of all. He had lots of
new friends...

...and a very
full tummy.

43

"Jolly night it's been," he murmured and began to snore.

"How will I get him home?" said the boy.

"I'll help," said George.
He gave the dragon a prod.

45

And they set off up the
hill arm-in-arm — the saint,
the dragon and the boy.

About this story

The Reluctant Dragon was first published over 100 years ago. The author, Kenneth Grahame, also wrote the famous children's story *The Wind in the Willows*.

Designed by Caroline Spatz
Digital manipulation: John Russell
Series editor: Lesley Sims
Series designer: Russell Punter

First published in 2009 by Usborne Publishing Ltd., Usborne House, 83-85 Saffron Hill, London EC1N 8RT, England. www.usborne.com
Copyright © 2009 Usborne Publishing Ltd.